W9-AVC-661

FEATURING CHARACTERS FROM ***PLANES*** AND

Designed by
TONY FEJERAN

Illustration directed by
JEAN-PAUL ORPIÑAS

Printed in the United States of America First Edition, 2014 10 9 8 7 6 5 4 3 2 1 ISBN 978-1-4231-7567-4

Library of Congress Control Number: 2014930989 G942-9090-6-14108

Visit www.disneybooks.com

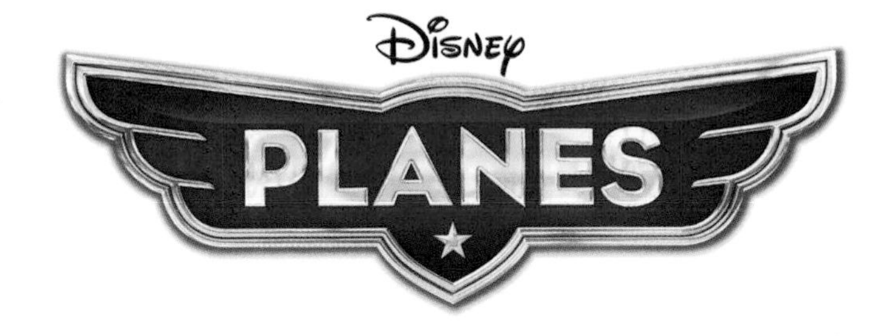

MEET THE PLANES

FEATURING CHARACTERS FROM *PLANES* AND

Written by **TODD GARFIELD** & **PAUL GERARD**
Illustrated by the **DISNEY STORYBOOK ART TEAM**

DISNEY PRESS
NEW YORK • LOS ANGELES

CONTENTS

Not so long ago, Dusty Crophopper spent his days dusting the corn crops of Propwash Junction with nutritious Vita-minamulch. Dusty liked being a crop duster, but he had a bigger dream in mind: Dusty Crophopper wanted to be a racer! However, Dusty soon discovered that dreams don't come true without a lot of help. While he was lucky enough to win his first race—the famous Wings Around The Globe Rally, Dusty was even luckier to make lifelong friends along the way.

Dusty returned to Propwash Junction as a racing champion! But when an unexpected fire shut down the town, Dusty knew he had to do whatever he could to help his friends. Soon, the crop duster turned racer was training to become a firefighter! The ace firefighting team at Piston Peak National Park taught the rookie everything they knew, and Dusty had a whole squadron of brave new friends!

Climb aboard, and meet all the amazing PLANES characters who've taught Dusty that friendship is the greatest adventure of all.

**As you read, be sure to check the PLANES GLOSSARY at the end of the book to learn the meaning of the technical terms that Dusty and his crew use each day.

PLANES

WELCOME TO PROPWASH JUNCTION

Propwash Junction is the perfect place for vehicles of all makes and models to call home. The endless acres of golden corn and wide open skies are just part of Propwash's charm. Whether you're looking for a tune-up at Chug and Dottie's Fill 'n' Fly service station or a comfortable hangar for the night at Brody & Barbara's Landing Zone Motel, you're sure to be taken care of in this quaint little town. Of course, now that Dusty has won the Wings Around The Globe Rally, visitors from all over the world flock to Propwash Junction to see the hometown of everyone's favorite racer.

CROP DUSTER DUSTY

Dusty has always been a plane with high hopes—literally. Crop duster by trade, this single-prop plane dreamed of soaring alongside his high-flying heroes in an international race. And the fact that he wasn't really built for competitive racing never deterred him from pursuing that dream. With help from his friends, Dusty took off on an adventure of a lifetime, going prop to prop with renowned racing champions in the Wings Around The Globe Rally. This underdog managed to face his fear of heights and outsmart the competition to take home the trophy in honor of dreamers everywhere!

SUPER-CHARGED DUSTY

When Dusty finally made it to Mexico after crashing into the ocean during one of the last legs of the rally, Dottie was able to rebuild him thanks to a generous contribution of spare parts by the other Wings Around The Globe participants. Super-Charged Dusty was able to fly to victory with the help of his racing friends: Ishani donated the propeller given to her by Ripslinger; El Chu brought out the wings from a T-33 Shooting Star jet aircraft; and Bulldog even tossed in his spare satellite navigation device.

HONORARY JOLLY WRENCHES DUSTY

After his triumph in the Wings Around The Globe Rally, Dusty was invited back to Skipper's old ship, the U.S.S. *Dwight D. Flysenhower.* There, Dusty was granted an honorary membership in the Jolly Wrenches squadron and he received a special paint job so he would look the part.

SKIPPER RILEY

A reclusive old navy Corsair, Skipper was once an ace flier and top instructor in the esteemed Jolly Wrenches squadron. However, an incident during a combat mission took him off the front lines and left him grounded for good. Skipper kept to himself for a long time, but his quiet life was turned upside down when an ambitious and persistent Dusty solicited his aerial expertise. Skipper and Dusty helped one another come to terms with their own fears and regrets, so they could take to the skies and fly higher than they ever thought possible.

SPARKY

Every war vet needs a die-hard supporter like Sparky. The loyal, eager-to-please forklift is always there to lend a helping wrench to Skipper. The two go way back—Sparky is all too aware of Skipper's troubled past and has a great deal of respect for the old Corsair. Therefore, no one was more excited than Sparky when Skipper was finally able to return to the skies he was built to fly.

FAN CLUB SPARKY

When Chug the fuel truck set up his Official Dusty Fan Club Web site, he never thought it would be successful enough to pay for the whole crew's trip to Mexico! Of course, having Dusty's biggest fan, Sparky, buy every souvenir really helped.

CHUG

Fuel truck Chug is a real guy's guy. He works hard as a co-owner of the Fill 'n' Fly, the local service station he shares with Dottie—and plays hard by indulging in his own fuel from time to time. He has a big personality and is a bold supporter of Dusty's high-flying endeavors. Indeed, he's not only Dusty's buddy; he's his original coach and biggest fan.

DOTTIE

Dottie is a forklift who co-owns and operates the Fill 'n' Fly service station with Chug. As Dusty's friend and mechanic, Dottie had once hoped to keep him safe by grounding his sky-high hopes in reality. She would remind Dusty that he wasn't built to race, and that for him to do so was downright dangerous. But when Dusty entered the Wings Around The Globe Rally, Dottie had no choice but to support her friend during his big adventure.

LEADBOTTOM

Leadbottom is a puttering old biplane and a grumbling taskmaster, a real tank-half-empty kind of guy. As the proprietor of Vita-minamulch, a special—albeit putrid—blend of vitamins, minerals, and mulch that works miracles when sprayed on crops, Leadbottom has no time for Dusty's far-fetched flights of fancy. There are too many crops to spray and not enough hours in the day to spray them. For Leadbottom, it's work first, then . . . well, work more.

MAYDAY

Feisty ol' Mayday has been Propwash Junction's fire and rescue truck for decades. He's always rarin' to go and eager to confront any emergency. However, he's lost some speed, his hoses are leaky, and he can't see very well. Luckily, fires in Propwash are rare.

WINGS AROUND THE GLOBE RALLY

With the desire to bring far-flung nations together, the first international air race was proposed twenty-nine years ago by the International Association of Racing Planes. This race had only three competitors, very little media coverage, and just one plane that actually completed the journey.

That is far from the international spectacle that Wings Around The Globe (WATG) is today, but it did establish the route, a rally system of timed race stages, and the countries that host each stage. Over the years, the number of competitors, the attendance, and the coverage have all grown. Now 136 nations compete in four time trials worldwide—one of which is the Lincoln Qualifier. The top five from each of these trials qualify to enter the final rally of twenty-one planes, including the previous year's champion. Racing Sports Network (RSN) has been providing complete coverage of the race for the last twelve years, giving millions of fans around the world the opportunity to cheer on their favorite racers each year.

RIPSLINGER (U.S.A.)

With more wins than he can count and an abundance of fans, Ripslinger is wings down the biggest name in air racing—and he knows it. Despite sky's-the-limit funding and state-of-the-art equipment, the world champion still doesn't play fair—especially when it comes to a small-town plane with zero racing experience. Dusty didn't belong in Ripslinger's sport, and his mere presence made the pro's fuel boil throughout the entire Wings Around The Globe Rally. Ripslinger was so desperate not to lose to the inexperienced crop duster that he had his underhanded sidekicks try to sabotage Dusty. But you know what they say: cheaters never prosper. And Dusty's ultimate win at the rally is proof.

KENNY DOOSAN

Performing full detail work and buffing out scratches are only minor examples of Kenny Doosan's duties as Ripslinger's head pitty. Kenny is a rolling warehouse of knowledge when it comes to the cutting-edge technology that keeps Ripslinger's engine at top performance.

NED & ZED

Team Ripslinger's bombastic racers Ned and Zed specialize in sabotage. Lacking the skills to actually outrace the competition, they simply eliminate it, propelling boss Ripslinger to victory every single time. Zed, a rowdy and reckless flier, and Ned, a strange bird himself, may not be the sharpest props in the hangar, but they have figured out how to draft off Ripslinger's fame.

BULLDOG (GREAT BRITAIN)

Bulldog has been racing longer than every other racer on the circuit. As the oldest and arguably wisest plane in the rally, he remembers a time before GPS, when real racers trusted their gyros and navigated by the stars. When it comes to racing, Bulldog believes it boils down to two qualities: good flying and sportsmanship. While the competition secretly wonders if the aging plane is past his prime, he flies his way onto the leaderboard again and again, proving that this Bulldog has lost none of his bite.

FORKSWORTH

Forksworth is the ultimate gentleplane's assistant. He has been with Bulldog for decades and taught the British racer everything he knows about etiquette, both on and off the course.

EL CHUPACABRA (MEXICO)

The intensely charming El Chupacabra is a legend in Mexico (just ask him). Powered by his passion for racing (not to mention the elusive Rochelle), this caped Casanova is anything but low-key; his booming voice and charismatic presence are as big as his oversized engine. His cohorts aren't really sure what is truth and what is delusion when it comes to El Chu, but one thing is beyond doubt: he races with a whole lot of heart and more dramatic flair than recommended at high altitudes.

RICARDO

It takes a special kind of pitty to assist a plane like El Chu . . . and Ricardo is just the vehicle for the job. From reading lines with El Chu for the racer's telenovela role to practicing *luchador* (wrestling) moves to fending off El Chu's adoring fans with said *luchador* moves, Ricardo has been forced to acquire quite a varied skill set.

ISHANI (INDIA)

The reigning Pan-Asian racing champion and pop star from India, Ishani is easy on the eyes, but ruthless in the skies. Thanks to her high-speed competitiveness and notable talent, she has amassed more than a billion loyal fans—including Dusty, who turned to her for guidance. Exotic and mysterious, Ishani is full of surprises, but she always has her eye on the prize.

RIYA

As a lifelong fan of Ishani, Riya was thrilled to become her pitty. Especially because, as an aspiring singer herself, Riya hopes to someday be invited to take on the role of backup singer in one of Ishani's famous music videos. Ishani might give Riya a shot if she would just come out and ask, instead of simply dropping hints all the time!

ROCHELLE (CANADA)

Rochelle is a tough racer and the pride of the Great White North. Always confident and capable, she got her start running mail to small towns in Quebec, picking up home remedies for mechanical maladies along the way. She also developed a knack for fast travel that ultimately inspired her to give air racing a try. Rochelle never looked back (this competitive contender doesn't need to). She is relentlessly pursued by charmer El Chupacabra, but steadfast Rochelle is much too focused on winning the race to return his affections.

ANNIE TWIST

Annie had dreams of seeing the world. But she never thought her dreams would become a reality until she met Rochelle. When the two met, Rochelle felt a connection—and decided to take Annie under her wing and bring her along on an amazing adventure.

INTERNATIONAL ROCHELLE

As the film PLANES played around the world, the character of Rochelle took on exotic new looks. In some countries, she even got a brand-new name!

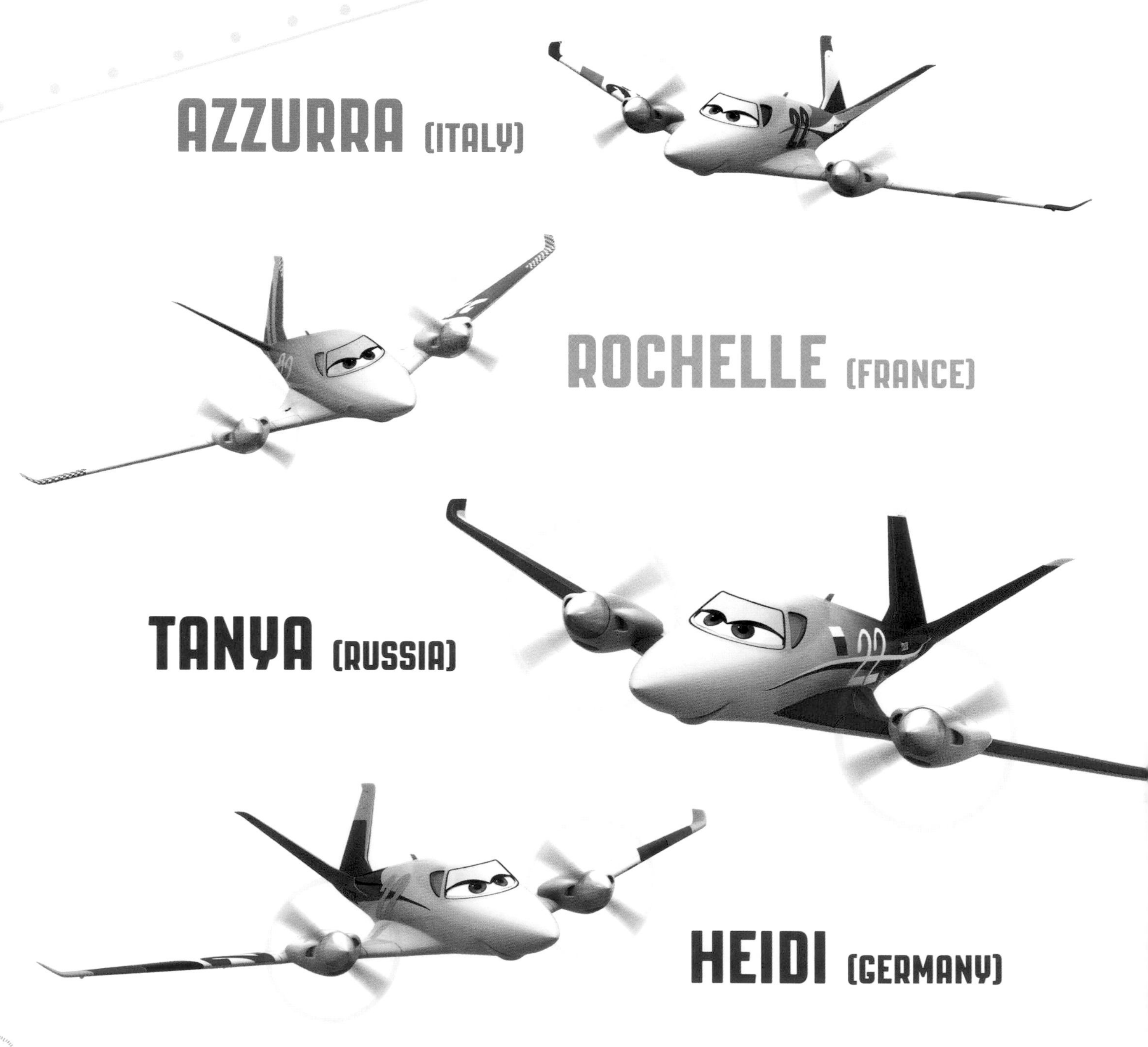

ROCHELLE (AUSTRALIA)

YUN YAN FEI (CHINA)

SAKURA (JAPAN)

CAROLINA (BRAZIL)

VECIHI (TURKEY)

Growing up in Turkey, Vecihi developed his famous Istanbul Power Dive, which he has used to surprise countless competitors on the final legs of races. Vecihi is hoping to use his classic move to surprise his competitors in this year's Wings Around The Globe Rally.

SAMIMI

Probably the friendliest vehicle on the circuit, Samimi makes an effort to meet each of his fellow pitties. He's always eager to invite them to visit Istanbul and promises to whip up a mean cup of Turkish petrol to get their motors really running.

ARTURO (ITALY)

Arturo finds it fitting that his name begins with "art." With immense pride in his Italian roots, Arturo doesn't just race—he creates a new masterpiece at each event by demonstrating the excellence of his metal aerostructure and the elegance of his precise engineering. With a 1,300-horsepower engine, his graceful moves are like delicate brushstrokes across the sky.

LIFTY LUCIANO

Italian pride runs strong in Lifty as well. This tough little pitty better not overhear you talking trash about his country, or his racer, for that matter. It's rumored that vehicles who cross good ol' Lifty find themselves sleeping with the submarines.

ANTONIO (SPAIN)

Antonio loved growing up in the rain-prone coastal region of Spain. He and his buddies flew in the rain nearly every day for Hispano Aviacion. Neither *lluvia*, nor *aguanieve*, nor *nieve* (rain, nor sleet, nor snow) kept them out of the sky. Antonio now thrives in extreme weather, seeking out races where conditions come into play. That's why racing fans say: "When there's rain, bet on the plane from Spain!"

SANCHO

Sancho became a racing pitty because he wanted to see the world . . . not the world's weather systems. He really wishes Antonio would pick sunnier races.

SUN WING (CHINA)

As a biplane, Sun Wing never thought that racing would be her ultimate profession. However, after she was discovered by the famous Chinese racing coach Nanchang, Sun Wing's notable skills took her straight onto the international racing circuit.

MA DÁ ZUI

Sun Wing isn't much of a talker, but her motormouth pitty speaks enough for the both of them. However, this isn't such a bad thing, as Ma Dá Zui also happens to be fluent in over fifty languages, making him an excellent international travel companion.

JOEY DUNDEE (AUSTRALIA)

Long-distance races are the strength of this Australian flier. That's because he got his start making supply runs to the deepest regions of the outback. Joey's high-aspect-ratio wings (like those of a glider or long-distance bomber) allow him to fly long distances with ease while using less power. Joey uses an ancient didgeridoo (pipe-like wind instrument) humming technique, taught to him by the locals of the outback, to help him conserve energy for sustained flight. When he isn't humming, Joey loves telling corny jokes.

WALLY ROO

In addition to his normal pitty duties, Wally is also the better half of Joey Dundee's comedy act. While he plays the straight man in all of Joey's bits, Wally actually writes most of their funny material.

MIGUEL (BRAZIL)

Having started as an acrobatic flier in the "Esquadrilha da Nevoeiro"—the Fog Squadron—Miguel knows how to carve a line through crowded airspace. But he doesn't just have moves—he has endurance, thanks to a lifetime of samba-ing the night away in his hometown of Rio, Brazil. And yet, no matter how much he burns the midnight oil, he's still raring to go when race time rolls around.

BRUNO

Although he's constantly traveling around the world with Miguel, Bruno always makes sure he's home in time to prepare for Carnival. He loves making crazy costumes to wear for the celebration. Miguel has fun trying to spot Bruno in the parade . . . the outfits are so elaborate he can't recognize his own pitty!

VAN DER BIRD (NETHERLANDS)

Back in the glorious 1920s and 1930s, the Dutch dominated the world of aviation. Van Der Bird races every day to restore the Netherlands' legacy. Training over sprawling tulip fields and beautiful windmills, Van Der Bird has a singular focus: to be the best. The Netherlands inspires him to soar through every race; the faster he flies, the sooner he can return to his beloved homeland.

GILLIS

Gillis left his puddle-jumper country airport home to get a job in the big city, starting as a baggage handler at Amsterdam Airport Schiphol. It wasn't long before this capable pitty was running the entire tarmac. Airport officials took notice; so, when Van Der Bird came looking for a pitty to assist him on his quest to restore racing pride to the Netherlands, they proudly recommended Gillis. It took their tarmac quite a while to recover from the loss, though!

GUNNAR VIKING (NORWAY)

Originally from Copenhagen, this Skandinavisk Aero champion started out as an air ambulance—flying medevac operations between hospitals in Helsingor and Stauning. With his sirens on, Gunnar Viking would make the 270-kilometer flight in just twenty minutes. This went unnoticed until a Copenhagen sports reporter calculated that this meant that Gunnar was flying 510 miles per hour between the two cities—five miles per hour faster than unlimited-class racers. That's when Gunnar Viking traded his sirens for racing stripes.

ULFBERHT

Ulfberht is among the mightiest of pitties. He claims his steel forks were forged in the fires of a volcano and can shatter the hardest materials on earth with a single blow. While impressive, these feats are all but entirely worthless on the racing circuit.

LITTLE KING (IRELAND)

Little King used to fly the mail route across the Derrynasaggart Mountains in County Cork, all the way to the border of County Kerry. With so many miles logged zigzagging his way across Ireland, Little King was clearly built to go the distance. Eager to see what was beyond the borders of his homeland, this little *eitleán* (airplane) entered the world of international racing.

JAN KOWALSKI (POLAND)

Fellow racers affectionately refer to Jan as the "Polish Prankster." His pistons are always firing up ways to mess with his pals—whether it's putting a stink bomb in their exhaust systems or attaching a "Buzz me!" banner to their tails. Savvy racers keep this trickster on their radar, so they don't end up as the rudder of his jokes.

ŻARCIK

Żarcik not only helps Kowalski prepare for his races; he helps him pull his pranks as well. This devious mastermind always knows where to find the props they need. And if he can't find them, he can make them. Żarcik is truly Kowalski's wingman when it comes to pranks . . . except when they are pranking each other!

TSUBASA (JAPAN)

Tsubasa is known as the "Ninja" because no one ever sees or hears him coming! Competitors fear the stealth of this master from Japan, who slices past them like an invisible warrior, eluding even their radar. His slick airframe produces little drag and nary a whisper—Tsubasa's propeller blades have brush-like trailing edges and are driven by a silenced engine, which reroutes its exhaust noise through his muffled intake. His unique "Shinobi style" of racing is based on illusion and misdirection—Tsubasa disappears into one cloud and emerges from another, leaving his opponents in a tailspin.

KAGE

Tsubasa couldn't have picked a better match for his stealthy style. Performing his tasks with ninja-like precision and efficiency, Kage's motto is "A job well done is a job done unseen." Of course, you'd have to find this elusive pitty first to hear him say this.

KOLYA IVANOV (RUSSIA)

In the coldest parts of the Siberian tundra, Kolya Ivanov started training for a career in racing. He often looks down on his competitors, but not because he's a snob. As a high-altitude racer, Kolya flies just above 60,000 feet. And with a maximum speed that has yet to even be declassified, he is most certainly a tough competitor to beat.

YELLOWBIRD (U.S.A.)

Originally from Wyoming, Yellowbird got involved in racing quite by accident. Immensely proud of his Native American heritage, Yellowbird would travel back and forth between western Wyoming and southeastern Montana to participate in the annual Cheyenne Nation Air Rodeo. It was at one of those rodeos that a Wings Around The Globe racing promoter noticed him and suggested that Yellowbird enter a regional air race. Yellowbird easily won that first race, and the rest is history.

FONZARELLI

Originally from the Midwest, Fonzarelli used racing to escape the mean runways of east Youngstown. Fonzarelli started out as a delivery plane for the local olive- and mineral-oil businesses; but at night, he would compete in illegal radio tower races. It was there that Fonzarelli learned about an open WATG-approved race in nearby Cleveland. He flew away from his past in Youngstown and never looked back.

RONNIE RIZZO

Originally a dock worker from the industrial flats along the Cuyahoga River, Ronnie Rizzo always had a knack for mechanics and enhancing engine performance. Ronnie met Fonzarelli at a race and decided to pursue his dream of running an aerial racing pit crew.

PACK RAT

Racer number 10 at the Lincoln Qualifier, Pack Rat used to fly cargo in and out of Spokane, Washington. Every year, 54,000 tons of cargo flies in and out of Spokane. Most of that work is left up to planes much larger than Pack Rat, but even small packages need a lift into the little towns in the area. That is where Pack Rat got her name . . . at least the "Pack" part of her name. Don't ask her about the "Rat" part. . . .

PISTON

Piston is a tenacious racer who found himself trying again at this year's Lincoln Qualifier. He is powered by a six-cylinder air-cooled inverted in-line engine. Because his engine is upside down in comparison to his competitors', he often suffers from a lack of fuel called "dry piston." This is similar to the feeling of running out of gas. Because he complained about it so much, his nickname became "Piston."

GORDON

Having already achieved great success in the world of acrobatic flying, Gordon decided to enter the world of competitive rally racing. Gordon's signature move is a reverse half Cuban Eight: starting from level flight, Gordon pulls into a 45-degree climb, performs a half roll while still climbing, and then completes five-eighths of a loop to level out again. It is far more exciting to watch than to read about.

JACKSON RILES

Like Dusty, Jackson Riles, was a first-timer at the Lincoln Qualifier. And like every racer, Jackson dreams of racing in the Wings Around The Globe Rally. Powered by a compact air-cooled horizontally opposed flat-four engine, Jackson Riles may not have the horsepower of his unlimited-class competitors, but he has enough passion to make up the difference.

LJH 86 SPECIAL

A very patriotic plane, LJH 86 Special was built in the cradle of liberty in Pennsylvania, hence his stars-and-stripes paint scheme. Although he failed to qualify, LJH 86 is a hard plane to keep grounded, and he will undoubtedly be back next year.

FIREBIRD

Racer number 16, Firebird, is a fast biplane out of Fresno and a force to be reckoned with. Firebird has raced in the the Lincoln Qualifier three times, and though she hasn't qualified to date, next year will be the "Year of the Firebird." Or at least that is what it says in her latest press release. . . .

HAMMER

When trucks "put the hammer down" it means they are going at maximum speed. Racer number 17, Hammer, is always going at maximum speed, which he prefers to call "terminal velocity." Whatever you call it, Hammer is fast. But after three failed attempts at qualifying, Hammer is starting to question his need for speed.

BRENT
MUSTANGBURGER

Brent Mustangburger is an American sports-broadcasting icon. With the self-proclaimed "best stall in the garage," the excitable 1964½ Ford Mustang's voice is widely considered one of the most recognizable in the history of sports television—and he is associated with some of the most memorable moments in modern sports.

COLIN COWLING

Affable blimp Colin Cowling attended the prestigious Zeppelin Broadcasting School and began his career as the play-by-play voice for the Pacific Coast Balloon Races. He got his big break when his local *Eye in the Sky in Sports* weekly recap show was noticed by producers at Racing Sports Network.

GRAHAM PAIGE

This little four-cylinder never thought that he would be waving the starting flag at the world's biggest air racing event. But when Graham got his chance, he took it—not only waving the green starting flag when the competitors raced east across the Atlantic, but also the checkered flag when the finalists returned from the west.

JUDGE DAVIS

Though they haven't seen each other in years, Judge Davis is actually an old friend of Skipper Riley's. They met back in basic flight school, where they were both instructors. When it came time to deploy, Skipper was sent west to the Pacific, while Davis went east to Europe. Davis became the commander of the famed Red Tail Squadron, which never lost a bomber on their escort missions. Now retired, Judge Davis is the top official in all of air racing.

FRANK

In airspace as busy as JFK's, it is important to keep aircraft at a safe distance from each other. That orderly flow also needs to be maintained when the planes are on the ground. Keeping the constant stream of vehicles moving safely is where Frank's team of air traffic controllers shine, making the countless split-second decisions look easy.

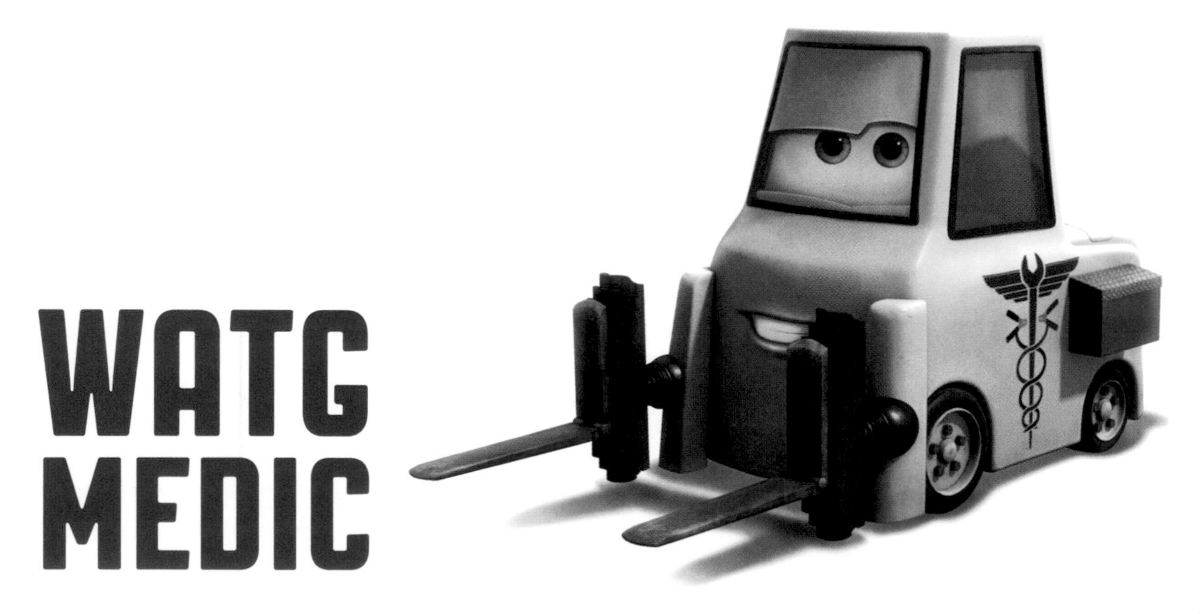

WATG MEDIC

At all the stops along the Wings Around The Globe Rally, there is a medic on call to assist with injured planes. As planes in need of assistance come into a checkpoint, it's up to the medic to determine which get help first in an emergency situation, based on the severity of their condition.

TRIPP

Tripp, a jet airliner, is short for Triple Seven or 777. His sleek exterior is distinguished by the vibrant stripes on his tail. Tripp first met Dusty Crophopper at JFK airport in New York, and the two have crossed paths several times since.

HARLAND

Harland has extensive knowledge of all ground operations at JFK. A pushback tractor, Harland helps move planes toward and away from terminal buildings and gates.

ROPER

This irascible race official delivers the rules for the North American Wings Around The Globe time trials with a matter-of-fact personality and a wry sense of humor. In fact, Roper never misses an opportunity to offer his own take on the events as they unfold. With sly remarks and colorful commentary, Roper is funny but firm in his dealings with the race and the racers.

WILLY KNIGHT

Driving Roper around is not a pleasant job, but someone has to do it. The race official isn't the most pleasant of passengers, as he gets motion sickness on long trips. Luckily, Willy can't really hear Roper complain when he is riding in the back.

FRANZ

Franz is a meek German minicar with a very special feature: he can fly! Without his wings, he's a mild-mannered superfan who would do anything for Dusty, including manning his personal Crop Watcher blog in an effort to build the rookie plane's fan base. Franz figures if an unknown crop duster can keep up with the best in the world, maybe his own high-flying dreams aren't so crazy after all.

VON FLIEGENHOSEN

With a flip of his doors, Franz's wings—and his airborne alter ego, von Fliegenhosen—emerge, turning the superfan into a brash, brazen, and fearless überfan. Von Fliegenhosen looks down on his "schpineless" four-wheeled counterpart, and his warring personalities don't see eye to eye on anything except the source of their inspiration: Dusty.

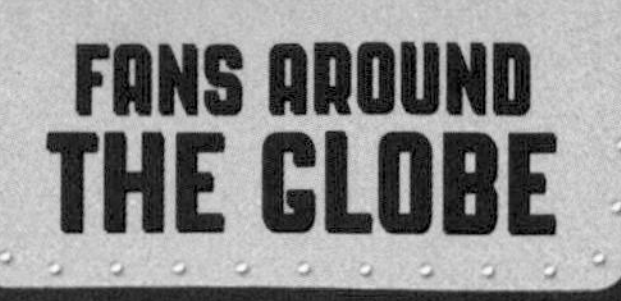

MORIMOTOR

Like all great sushi chefs, Morimotor has spent nearly a lifetime training under one of the best. For Morimotor, it was master sushi chef Jirozowa, who owned the most renowned and haughtiest sushi restaurant in all of Japan. Looking for a bit more fun, Morimotor finally opened his own "sushiria" and sports bar. Loyal patrons eagerly gather at Morimotor's to watch the Wings Around The Globe Rally and enjoy his infamous Hot Flight Rolls.

Linde loves moving things around; that's why he got into moving. Linde can lift 18,000 pounds of steel or feathers or anything else you might want him to move. He loves diesel, but he can alternate between multiple fuels—even natural gas if that's all that's available.

K. MATSU

Along with corn, rice is the most important grain the world produces. As a skilled farmer, K. Matsu harvests rice with tender loving care—and without ever dropping a single tiny grain!

ALEJANDRO

Being a mariachi in Shanghai is a tough, lonely existence, considering the fact that there are only thirteen Mexican restaurants in a city of twenty-four million vehicles. Alejandro loves nothing more than a performance, so when El Chu asked for his help in serenading Rochelle, it was the highlight of his career!

PRAMATH

Pramath joined the Kashmir Railway to get away from it all. More than anything, this train hoped to find a quiet, remote place to live, and trekking through the Himalayas seemed the perfect solution. He found the quiet rides through the mountain tunnels of the Pir Panjal range peaceful and therapeutic; that is, until he nearly had a head-on collision with Dusty Crophopper.

TENZIN

Originally from western China, the mini monk truck Tenzin now lives in Tibet. Although, because Tenzin believes in recycling, it is possible that his parts may have lived in Tibet several times before. . . .

ENGLISH PUB FANS

There is no "bower" or "aggro" allowed in Ye Olde Knuckle Head; that kind of hooliganism is not welcome—just good old-fashioned rooting for the local football club, the Rovers, and, of course, watching the Wings Around The Globe Rally on the telly.

HELGA

Helga has been tending the bar at the Munich Oil Hall for as long as she can remember. In her festive green dirndl (traditional barmaid's dress), she's happy to serve you a stein of oil and the best soft pretzel around.

NAVY BUDDIES

If it weren't for the help of Dusty's fans in the navy, he would have never made it across the Pacific. Whether it was his Jolly Wrenches emblem (which Sparky and Skipper gave him after he completed his training) or his immense courage, something about Dusty set him apart from the rest of the pack and earned him a huge following on the U.S.S. *Dwight D. Flysenhower*.

ECHO & BRAVO

Armed with stellar instincts, incredible aerial abilities, and outstanding service records, Bravo and Echo are two of the Jolly Wrenches' top troops. These fighter jets happen to be avid air racing fans, too, with a special affinity for Dusty, who's adopted their Jolly Wrenches insignia. And as far as the racers are concerned, it doesn't hurt to have a couple of soldiers nearby should any plane falter under the immense pressure of the world's most rigorous rally.

U.S.S. *DWIGHT D. FLYSENHOWER*

A revered aircraft carrier, the U.S.S. *Dwight D. Flysenhower* travels all over the world, which is easy with 260,000 horsepower at your disposal. As the at-sea home of the Jolly Wrenches squadron, this ship cruises across the sea at over thirty knots. More impressively, he can ride the seven seas for up to twenty-five years without a fill-up! Talk about great gas mileage. . . .

FLYSENHOWER DECKHANDS

Maintaining operations on the flight deck of the U.S.S. *Dwight D. Flysenhower* takes an amazing amount of planning and well-choreographed actions. In order to keep track of the responsibilities of each player in this colorful ballet of helpers, the crew have color-coded paint jobs that identify their roles.

GREEN DECKHAND

Green deckhands are the catapult and arresting gear crew. They are responsible for the equipment that launches and stops the planes taking off from and landing on the *Flysenhower*. They also handle cargo and ground support equipment (GSE).

PURPLE DECKHAND

Nicknamed "the Grapes," the purple deckhands manage the different grades of aviation fuels and make sure that the planes are adequately refueled before takeoff.

RED
DECKHAND

The red deckhands handle the ordnance—missiles and bullets—for the planes, as well as work as the crash and salvage crew. They assist in recovering any vehicle that lands in the water. Their red color warns the rest of the crew that they may be carrying explosives as they go about their jobs of rearming the planes and helicopters.

BLUE
DECKHAND

The blue deckhands are the plane handlers, operating the elevators and ferrying the planes around the deck when the planes are not under their own power. They also deliver messages to planes and other crew members.

WALTER O'WHEELY

A career navy medic, Walter O'Wheely first worked on the U.S.S. *Saratoga* and the U.S.S. *Enterprise*, before meeting Dusty on the U.S.S. *Dwight D. Flysenhower*. In fact, it was during his time on the *Saratoga* that Walter oversaw the rescue of Dusty's friend Skipper after he crashed in the ocean.

CAPTAIN STINGER

Captain Tom Stinger is the executive officer (XO), and second in command, of the *Flysenhower*. He commands all the planes and helicopters assigned to the ship, including Echo and Bravo. Stinger spends most of his time managing flight operations from the radar room of the *Flysenhower*, where he can get a complete picture of both the deck operations and the airspace around his command.

LANDING SIGNAL OFFICER

The landing signal officer (LSO) is responsible for bringing incoming aircraft safely aboard the *Flysenhower*. He works closely with flight operations and the XO, Captain Stinger. Originally, the LSO would stand up on deck giving visual signals to the incoming planes. However, with the invention of the Fresnel lens optical landing system, nicknamed "the ball," the LSO is able to stay safely off the runway. The new optical landing system allows the incoming aircraft to judge their relationship to the deck through a series of lights.

AIRCRAFT HANDLING OFFICER

The aircraft handling officer directs all operations of the *Flysenhower*'s catapult, which can accelerate a plane from a dead standstill to 160 knots in two seconds. The aircraft handling officer on the *Flysenhower* is painted yellow to keep him distinct from his crew of green deckhands on the catapult and arresting gear crew.

HECTOR VECTOR

An integral member of the Mexican coast guard, Hector Vector is called on for only the most daring rescue missions. Hector and his rescue diver are both part of the special service operatives assigned to rescue downed aircraft at sea. This work is both daring and dangerous, and it takes a special kind of helicopter to perform these rescue missions. Thankfully, Hector is just that kind of chopper.

RESCUE DIVER

"That Others May Live" is the slogan of the rescue divers. Also known as pararescue divers, these special service operatives are tasked with the recovery and medical treatment of crew in both combat and natural disaster situations. The rescue divers have been called in to rescue planes, ships, and even spacecraft lost at sea.

PLANES:
FIRE &
RESCUE

PISTON PEAK FIREFIGHTERS

Responding to fire emergencies is the thankless job of the Piston Peak Firefighters. They serve and safeguard all of the visitors and property of Piston Peak National Park. With 3,468 square miles of forests and over three million visitors annually, it is an immense responsibility. Piston Peak National Park is kept safe year round by the ground crews, structural engines, and the air attack team.

AIR ATTACK TEAM

The idea of fighting fires with aircraft was first proposed in 1931. However, it wasn't until 1955 that firefighters began recruiting agricultural planes to assist them. From that moment forward, air attack teams joined ground crews to fight all remote fires. The Piston Peak Air Attack Team fearlessly protects the vast 2.2 million acres of forests, mountains, grassy flats, and glacial-cut valleys that constitute the park.

BLADE RANGER

Blade is the leader of the Piston Peak Air Attack Team. A veteran fire-and-rescue helicopter, he is an all-purpose aircraft equipped with a drop tank and hoist. Flying at 120 knots under a maximum cruising altitude of 13,500 feet, Blade is a tough and demanding air boss with a wry sense of humor. Earlier in his life, he was known as "Blazin' Blade" and played a rescue chopper on the hit TV show *CHoPs* (California Helicopter Patrol). After the tragic loss of his onscreen partner, Blade struggled with his purpose in life; however, he soon got a second chance when he trained to become a real fire-and-rescue helicopter. Now, instead of pretending to save lives, Blade saves 'em for real.

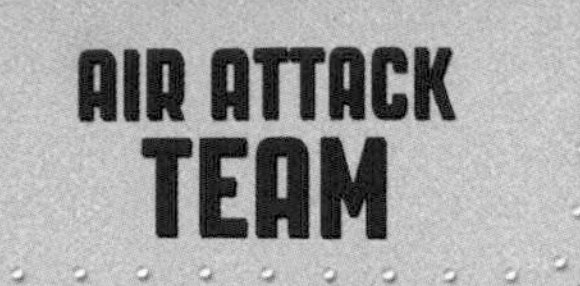

RACING DUSTY

After his underdog win at the prestigious Wings Around The Globe Rally, this crop duster turned racer flew back to his hometown of Propwash Junction as a hero (with a new paint job to boot!). Dusty was truly living his dream of being a professional racer; however, after he seriously injured himself during training one day, it seemed like Dusty's racing days were over for good. So when an unexpected fire threatened to shut down the town, Dusty decided to help out his friends and explore a new direction for his life by training with the aerial firefighters at Piston Peak Air Attack Base.

DUSTY
WITH PONTOONS

Maru attached pontoons to Dusty's fuselage, allowing him to scoop water from the surface of the lakes and rivers within Piston Peak National Park. The pontoons serve dual purposes: they not only scoop and store the water for firefighting, they are also buoyant enough to allow Dusty to land on and take off from the surface of the water. This modification makes Dusty a perfect addition to the Piston Peak Air Attack Team.

FIREFIGHTER DUSTY

When Dusty finally earned his certification from Blade, he became an official air attack SEAT, or single-engine air tanker. In honor of this promotion, Dusty was painted with the signature paint scheme of the Piston Peak Air Attack Team.

LIL' DIPPER

Lea "Lil' Dipper" Levine is a super scooper, able to skim lakes and collect water to drop on fires. She loves to watch air racing and has a huge crush on WATG champion Dusty Crophopper, so she's stunned and thrilled when he shows up at Piston Peak. Outgoing and spirited, she's always full of positive energy and enthusiasm. She's also a tough and fearless firefighter, able to drop 1,620 gallons of water on a fire. Before coming to Piston Peak, Dipper hauled cargo up in Alaska; like everyone on the team, she found a second life as a firefighter. Her best friend on the team is Windlifter, as she nicely counterbalances his reserved demeanor.

WINDLIFTER

Windlifter is a heavy-lift helicopter capable of hoisting dozens of trees or a huge tank of retardant. He is the strongest of the team, able to lift a payload up to 20,000 pounds. He is also an American Indian who is very knowledgeable about fire folklore. His connection to nature allows him to sense fires before they've even started. A skilled and dedicated firefighter, Windlifter never backs down from any mission. He was a lumberjack in his former career and became a firefighter out of a desire to help others. His best friend is Dipper, whose bubbly personality is the complete opposite of his soft-spoken disposition.

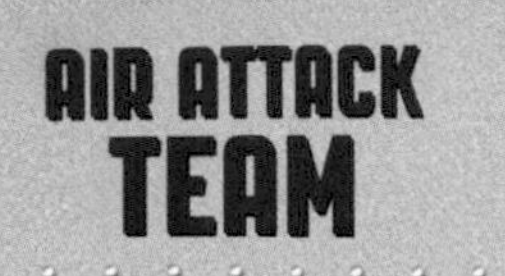

CABBIE

A jolly old ex-military transport plane, Cabbie McHale used to drop airborne jeeps behind enemy lines back in Korea. But after retiring from the military, he flew dull transport routes and found life to be unfulfilling. Then he discovered firefighting and his zest for life returned. For him, dropping smokejumpers is the closest thing to dropping soldiers into combat. Cabbie has a payload of 10,000 pounds and a maximum takeoff weight of 74,000 pounds—enough to carry all the smokejumpers and their gear as far as 2,000 miles.

MARU

Maru is the mechanic tug at the Piston Peak Air Attack Base. Friendly with a sarcastic sense of humor, he's been around a long time and has seen many firefighters come and go. A huge pack rat, Maru has filled his service hangar with racks of old parts and machinery, organized in a way that only he understands. Since everything on the base is repurposed equipment, he has become a professional at modifying or fabricating almost anything the team needs. When he's finished a repair, you will almost always hear him shout, "It's better than new!"

PATCH

Patch is not only in charge of the smoke reports that come in from the emergency communication center, she is also Piston Peak Air Attack's meteorologist and DJ. Her collection of vinyl records is famous among music collectors. She and Maru are the only members of the air attack crew who don't go out to fight the fires, so that leaves her time to perfect her playlist and keep the glass windows on her lookout tower spotless.

DYNAMITE

Dynamite is the strong and sassy female leader of the smokejumpers . . . so named because you don't wanna set her off. Equipped with a radio, she calls the shots on the ground and makes requests for drops from the aircraft. Though she rules over her gang with a sharp tongue, she's also fiercely protective of them.

PINECONE

Pinecone can name every tree in the forest. A southern, easygoing soul, she got her nickname because she loves to study pinecones (although she always puts them back). More importantly, she is equipped with a rake tool to clear brush and debris from the front line of any fire she meets.

AVALANCHE

A burly, friendly bulldozer who sorely lacks an "inside voice," this loud talker supposedly got his name by causing a massive avalanche with his shouting. However, Avalanche staunchly claims he was nowhere *near* that snowbank. . . .

BLACKOUT

Tough and overeager for action, Blackout was given his call sign when he accidentally sawed down an electrical line and cut power to the lodge for three weeks. As a result of the electric shock he received during the incident, he now has trouble remembering details.

DRIP

An outgoing dude who's always leaking oil, Drip is an off-the-grid kind of thinker. He likes to live in the extreme: extreme sports, extreme music, and extreme makeovers. He uses a skid-steer claw to clear fallen trees and brush.

CHoPs

Created in 1977 by executive producer Rick Rotor, *CHoPs* was a television show about two California Helicopter Patrol choppers, Nick Lopez and Blade Ranger, who fought crime over the busy freeways of Los Angeles.

NICK "LOOP'N" LOPEZ

By 1978, Nick Lopez was America's favorite helicopter cop. He was the troublemaking macho young officer who contrasted well with his by-the-book, levelheaded partner, Blade Ranger. Nick got the nickname "Loop'n" from his signature inside loop, which no other helicopter could perform.

"BLAZIN'" BLADE RANGER

Nick's partner, "Blazin'" Blade Ranger, was always keeping him out of trouble. A handsome, straitlaced helicopter officer, Blade often had to make excuses for his partner's rambunctious behavior, especially when their commanding officer, Sergeant Graeter, was on their backs.

SERGEANT "RHODEY" RHODES GRAETER

Gruff but lovable, Sergeant Graeter spent most of his time either busting Nick and Blade or giving them fatherly advice. As the commanding officer of the California Helicopter Patrol for twelve years, Rhodey thought he had seen it all . . . yet Nick always managed to find new ways to surprise his boss, both good and bad.

ZED CUSTARD

With 1,600 cubic feet of temperature-controlled storage space, Zed Custard is very good at keeping his precious cargo of doughnuts fresh. But Zed's doughnuts are not just any doughnuts; they're Winch's Donuts. Headquartered on the West Coast, Winch's is one of the largest distributors of doughnuts. Popular with all branches of law enforcement, these doughnuts are a filling treat day or night . . . and Zed is proud to be carrying only the best.

CHUCK SHOCKS

Fast-drivin', rubber-burnin' Chuck Shocks doesn't want any trouble from the police, yet he always seems to find it. It might be that Chuck doesn't think the rules of the road apply to him or that he feels that they are more *guidelines* than actual rules. Whatever the misunderstanding is, Chuck is just one moving violation away from the impound lot.

PEGGY & PINTA

Although it was only a drive-on role for one episode of *CHoPs*, Peggy and her sister Pinta made the most of their fifteen minutes of fame. They did commercials for their hometown furniture warehouse, were grand marshals of the Fourth of July parade, and even received the key to the city—which Peggy and Pinta agreed to pass back and forth each month, until the mayor asked for it back.

PISTON PEAK NATIONAL PARK

Established by an 1872 bill signed into law by President Teddy Rolls-Roycevelt, Piston Peak was the first national park in the United States. The park is known for its many iconic geological features, such as Gasket Geyser, Augerin Canyon, and—of course—towering high above V-6 Valley, the magnificent Piston Peak.

CAD SPINNER

Park superintendent Cad Spinner is a luxury sport-utility vehicle who's better suited to a country club than the country. Cad is so self-centered that he rarely hears the other side of a conversation. Profits are more important to him than safety, so it's no surprise that he's shifted a large chunk of the firefighters' budget to his lodge restoration project to boost tourism. He will do anything to protect his precious lodge, even at the expense of the rest of the park and its guests.

ANDRÉ

Serving all the needs of the Piston Peak Fusel Lodge's guests is André the concierge. Originally from France, André went to the famous Les Clefs d'Or School in Paris. If you want it, André can get it. If he can't get it, André knows the person who *can* get it. It is his business to know these things; he's the concierge!

OL' JAMMER

A trustworthy tour bus at Piston Peak for seventy-two years, Ol' Jammer knows more about the park than any other vehicle ever built. He's familiar with every trail, every stream, every rock, and every tree. He's seen many visitors come and go, and can recite the history of the park along with facts and figures about its flora and fauna. A gentle soul and a calming voice when danger strikes, Ol' Jammer is still strong and capable despite his age. He will gladly risk his life to protect his beloved park and those who come to enjoy it.

SECRETARY OF THE INTERIOR

The Secretary of the Interior has many responsibilities, but none is more important than overseeing the national parks. Hailing from the mountains of the west, this rugged outdoorsman loves being in nature. He spends most of his time away from his office, visiting the national forests and parks and helping to spread the message of conservation.

PULASKI

Pulaski is Piston Peak's structural engine, which means that he is responsible for protecting all the buildings and wooden bridges inside the park. With a two-thousand-gallon polypropylene tank, Pulaski is very matter-of-fact about his abilities: he can pump water at one thousand gallons per minute from his own tank or from the hydrants located throughout the park. Pulaski's biggest responsibility is protecting the renovated Fusel Lodge: seven stories tall, seven hundred feet long, every inch of it made of wood.

RAKE

Assistant fire officer and structural engine compatriot, Rake is always at Pulaski's side. He is aware of the immense responsibility of keeping the park's buildings protected and is always watchful for potential danger.

RANCE COLDSTART

Rance Coldstart has been a ranger at Piston Peak for twenty years. As a botany student and a fan of hiking and camping, this line of work seemed "natural." Rance is responsible for educating the public about Piston Peak's wildlife and geological formations, as well as protecting the park and its visitors.

WINNIE & HARVEY

This loving RV couple is returning to Piston Peak National Park, where they celebrated their honeymoon fifty years ago. Harvey and Winnie met when Harvey was the manager of an RV tire store and Winnie was his showroom model. Though they may occasionally bicker, their love is as strong as it was the day they met. Their goal? To find the spot where they had their first kiss, of course!

MUIR

The Piston Peak Railway transports millions of visitors to the Fusel Lodge every year. This is a huge job, and it takes a big engine; thankfully, Muir can handle the challenge. With enough coal, he can pull an astounding 18,000 tons of railcars behind him! With that much power, he'll be coming around the mountain just fine.

NEWLYWEDS
VINNIE & VERA

Having just exchanged their wedding valves, Vinnie and Vera came to Piston Peak on their honeymoon. Being hybrids, they both wanted a suite on the lodge's low-emissions floor. The couple is eager to see the sights of the park . . . they just haven't gotten around to it yet.

STEVE MARIOTTI

Steve's two major loves in life are the New York Crankies and air racing. In fact, he is such a loyal fan, he has never missed a single game or race. Such devotion keeps him on the road most of the year, which means that his cell phone is his lifeline. So you can just imagine Steve's delight at having *the* Dusty Crophopper record his outgoing message!

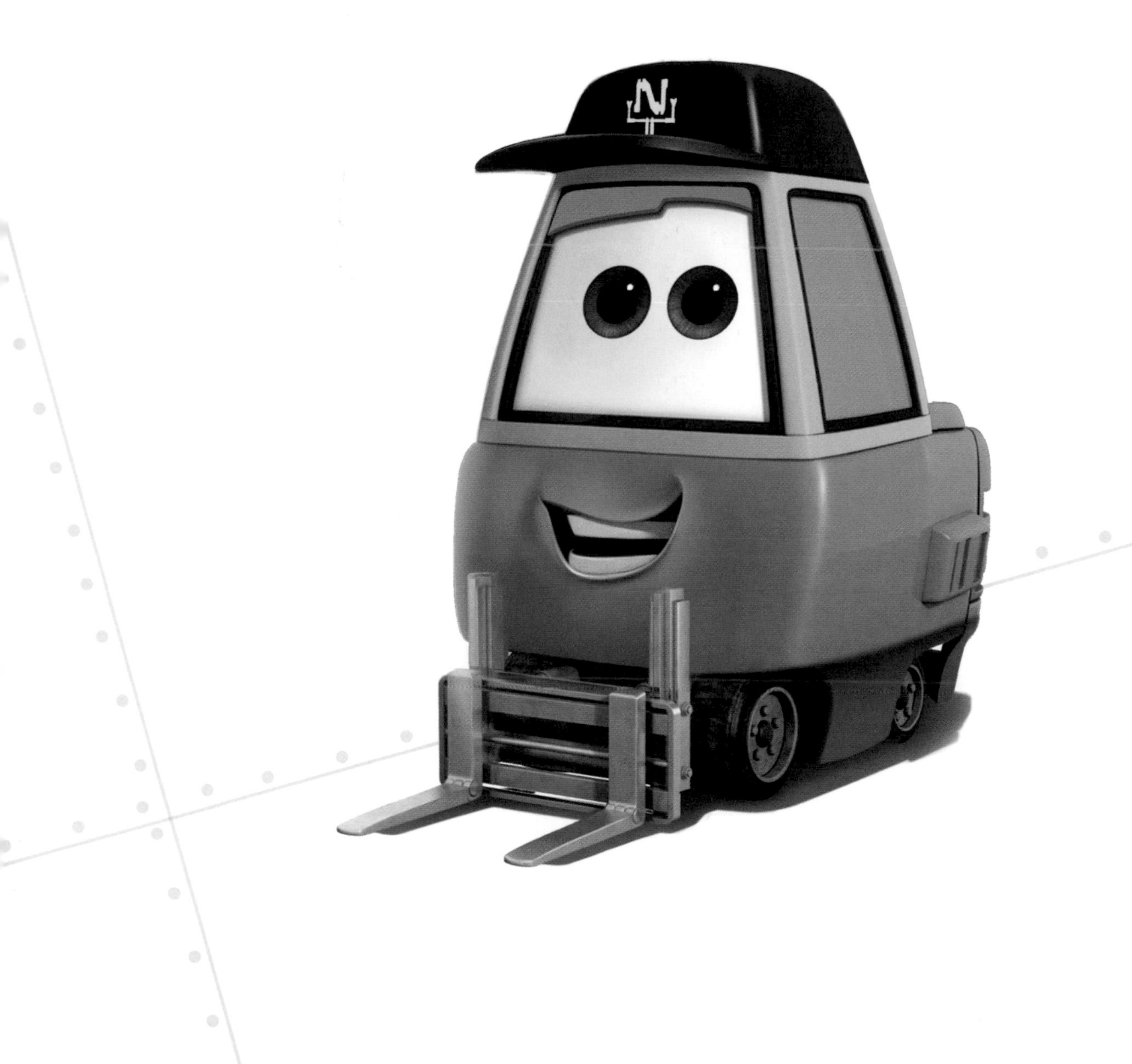

TED YALE

Ted Yale is a bellhop at Piston Peak's Fusel Lodge. He had been hoping to get the position of doorman, but as it turned out, all the lodge doors are automatic. Luckily, Ted has established himself as the best bag man in the hotel.

SYLVIA HYSTER

Whether it is mixing up a double clutch latte or foaming a cabuccino, Sylvia Hyster is the queen of the steam spout. This beatnik Piston Perk barista has learned more about coffee beans than any mere mortal will ever know. When she's not fixing up a caramel Macktruckiato, she is writing new verses for her next slam poetry competition.

BOAT
REYNOLDS

Well known for his roles as a good ol' boat who bucks authority, Boat Reynolds is an accomplished actor, director, and voice artist who started out as a star athlete. He was an all-conference boat racer in college when an injury ended his professional racing aspirations. Instead of becoming a police boat like his father, he went to New York to pursue acting. Now he is America's favorite leading boat!

MARTY STATLER

A member of the rock band the Pinheads, Marty had been off-roading all throughout Piston Peak National Park when he arrived at the newly renovated Fusel Lodge for the evening. Eager to check into a room after his long hike, mud-covered Marty was puzzled about why Cad Spinner would make him use the service entry instead of rolling through the main entrance. . . .

BO METHEUS

Bo Metheus admired the workmanship of the impressive ice sculpture of the renovated Fusel Lodge from the moment he saw it sitting in the lobby. His admiration soon turned to coveting, and when the fire alarms sounded, Bo saw an opportunity to take what he most desired. But by the time Bo got home, the sculpture he carried forty-seven miles through burning forests was barely large enough to chill a glass of water, proving once again that crime does not pay.

D.O.N.

Originally designed for the military, this housekeeper was adapted to clean floors using intelligent adaptive mapping technology. Known as D.O.N. (dirt and odor neutralizer), it hunts down bacteria, dust, and grime with extreme prejudice. With a patented four-stage process, the housekeeper locates dirt, stalks it, tricks the dirt into thinking it can't see it, and then eliminates it without mercy.

TOUR BUSES

Getting millions of visitors in and out of Piston Peak National Park is a huge task, but the Piston Peak Tour Buses are up to the job. Measuring eleven feet high and forty-six feet long, these stainless steel and fiberglass motor coaches carry passengers in climate-controlled comfort. Their seamless windows allow for the best possible views, which is important given the many magnificent vistas in Piston Peak.

CHRIS COMPASS

LINUS LINES

TRUDY TRAILWAY

VALERIE VISTAVIEW

DEER

BUCK AND DOE

These truly majestic vehicles are found in abundance on the plains of Piston Peak National Park. The males have headlight antlers, which they use to impress the females. Lucky park visitors may witness a "brights battle," where males face off, trying to blind any brave young bucks who step up to challenge them for their territory . . . or their ladies.

RED-PROPPED
BALSA AND BABY THRUSH

While the thrush species can be spotted in a variety of woods, the red-propped balsa thrush is among the rarest variety because of its fragile nature. Found mainly in the forests of Piston Peak National Park, the balsa thrush tries to conserve its energy by gliding on the valley updrafts. A thrush will only engage its propeller when absolutely necessary, as they are highly susceptible to rubber band snap.

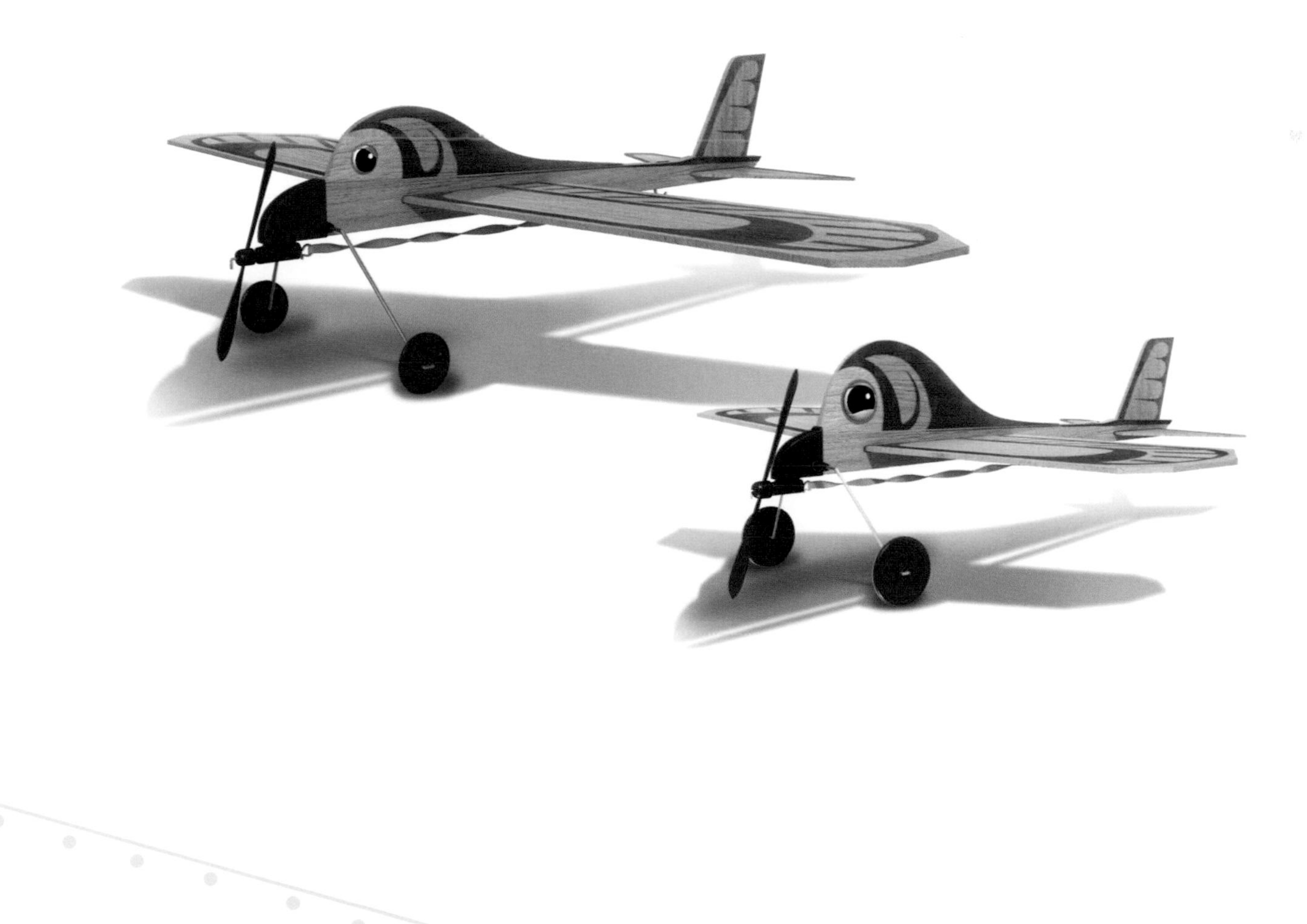

RETURN TO PROPWASH JUNCTION

After Dusty became certified as a single-engine air tanker (SEAT), and Dottie upgraded Mayday with modern firefighting equipment, Propwash Junction was officially reopened for air traffic. The Corn Festival went off without incident, and everyone was able to celebrate having a modern fire department to keep them safe.

RYKER

As an air safety investigator for the Transportation Management Safety Team (TMST), Ryker not only lives by the book, he *wrote* the book on airport accident investigations. The TMST is an independent federal agency charged with the task of investigating aviation accidents, as well as significant accidents involving other large vehicles, including trains and boats.

KURTZ

Kurtz is Ryker's right-hand forklift and one of the fastest note takers for the TMST. He mastered shorthand and has been taking copious notes ever since. Kurtz originally aspired to be a court reporter, but he never became proficient with the stenotype machine. So when he got the opportunity to take notes in the field for the TMST, he jumped at the chance to put his speedy skills to use!

BARBARA & BRODY ENID

Barbara and Brody are the owners and managers of the Landing Zone Motel in Propwash Junction. Brody is a durable, robust, and easy-flying kind of plane, whereas Barbara is more refined and direct. Barbara really runs things at the Landing Zone, but Brody denies this fact whenever she isn't around.

CARL "CRANKY" CASE

Since the beginning of air racing, Planezoil has been synonymous with superior quality oil. Carl "Cranky" Case ,the Planezoil delivery truck, is very proud of that heritage. The original air racing oil, Planezoil was a formula of different engine oil viscosities that mechanics simply called "plane's oil." Over time, the name for the formula stuck and became just "Planezoil." With a cargo capacity of 16,000 pounds, Carl travels throughout the Midwest delivering to mechanics and engineers like Dottie who swear by Planezoil.

ALICE

THE WAITRESS

Alice Brock has been working at Honkers almost as long as it has been open. Originally hired for her agreeable attitude and bright outlook, Alice grew out of both somewhere over the years. Thankfully, though, she still keeps the customers happy.

FLAP

Flap is a Honkers regular. He fancies himself a ladies' man but, to be honest, Flap has never talked to one longer than sixty seconds—which is probably for the best, considering that Flap runs out of clever things to say after a minute or so. . . .

KITT LIFT

Kitt has larger tires, axles, and suspension than most trucks. He also has a bigger engine. Whether Kitt is mud-bogging, off-roading, flying off jumps, or spinning on freestyle courses, he is doing it big. Kitt enjoys riding over giant rocks, trees, and anything else in his way.

SHARPES

When Sharpes pulls into Honkers for a cool drink, he never has what the other planes are having. Sharpes likes his drinks with tropical colors, a tangy aftertaste, and most important of all, a little umbrella on top.

GREG & MEG

Greg and Meg met at Honkers when they picked the same song on the jukebox: B17, "Runway Romance." After hearing the same song played twice in a row, they discovered they had more than just musical taste in common: they had both worked in construction, and neither likes to floss. It really was inevitable that they would end up together.

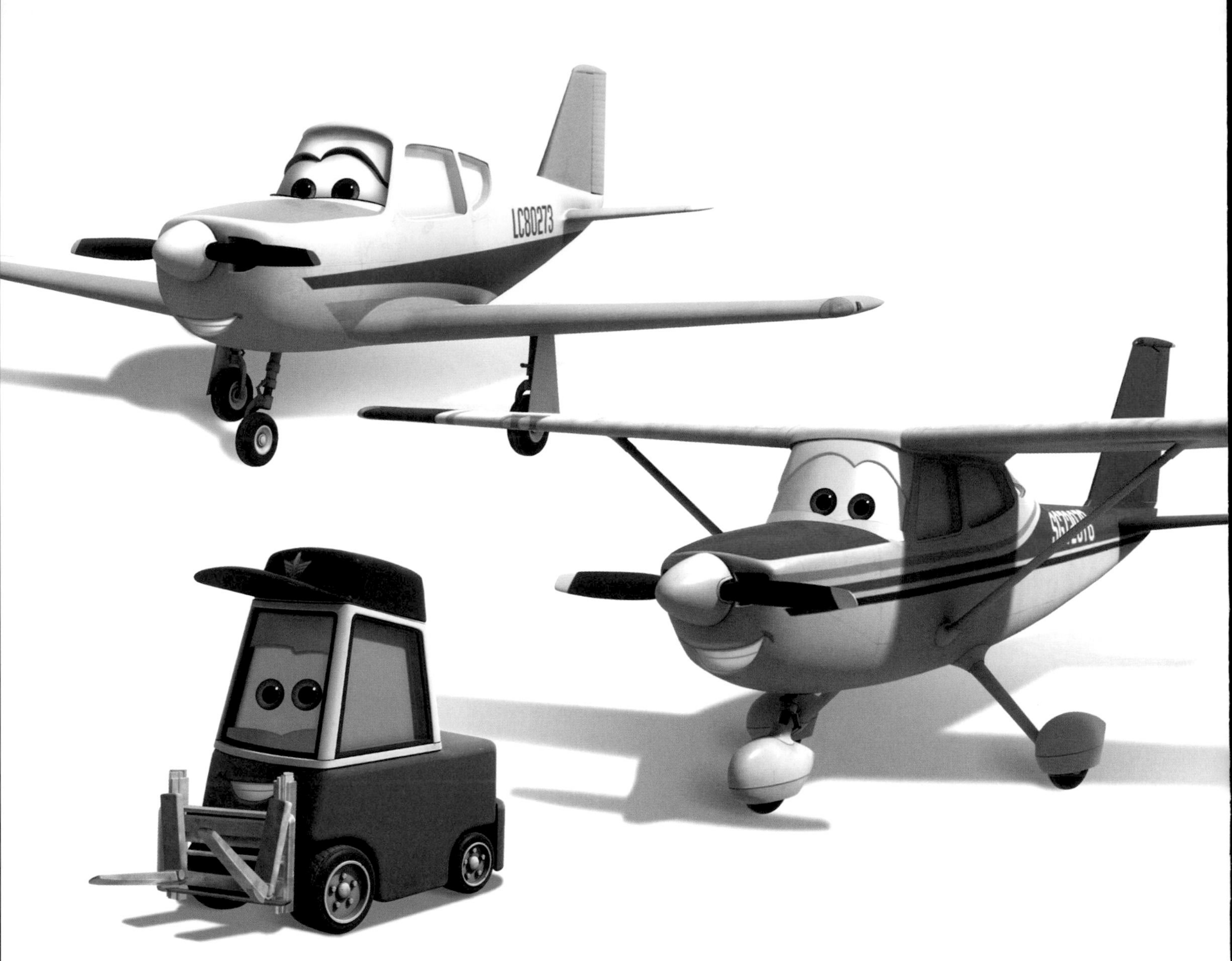

HONKERS REGULARS

The Honkers regulars know that this place is more than just a honky-tonk club. It isn't rowdy or loud, and there's no mechanical combine bucking customers into the air. Honkers is just a great place to hang out with friends.

TEX, MILLIE, & LUKE

By day they come from all walks of life; come nighttime, these friends fall into sync, as if the music itself is coursing through their fuel lines. They live for country line dancing, and Honkers is the place to get their stomp and shuffle on. While the Two Tire, Combustion Slide, and Hoedown Towdown are old favorite dances, nothing gets their engines running like a good ol' honky-tonk rendition of "Cotton-Eyed Joe-lopy."

PJFD MAYDAY

The Propwash Junction Fire Department has never looked better! With a brand-new prescription windshield, a new suspension, new lighting, and state-of-the-art firefighting equipment, Mayday is ready for any emergency that might arise. More importantly, though, Dusty's friend and fellow firefighter has a new lease on life.

CHUG

AS CORN COLONEL

Being Corn Colonel for Propwash Junction's annual Corn Festival is not just an honor; it is an immense responsibility. The Corn Colonel acts as judge at the annual "Aww, Shucks" corn-shucking contest and grand marshal at the Corn Festival parade, escorts the Corn Queen to the yearly Corn Festival air show, and is a spokesvehicle for greater corn awareness throughout the rest of the one-year reign.

SPARKY

AS PRIVATE NIBLET

Though not as immense a responsibility as Corn Colonel, the role of Private Niblet in the annual Corn Festival is still very important. As Private Niblet, Sparky attends to the Corn Colonel's needs throughout the festival. Also, in the unfortunate event that the Corn Colonel, the Lieutenant Colonel of Corn, the Major Bushel, and the Captain Maize all cannot perform their duties, Private Niblet would ascend to the role of Corn Colonel.

KATE (AKA THE CORN LADY)

Kate loves corn. No. Seriously. She really loves corn. Her hangar is filled with the stuff in every form: corncob candles, corn-husk bouquets, corn-oil paintings of corn. She even keeps ears of corn as pets . . . and feeds them popcorn. No one was more upset than her when the Corn Festival was temporarily canceled. She still hasn't taken off her costume . . . from last year!

Acrobatic flying: high-flying spins, loops, and rolls; also called "aerobatics."

Aeronautics: the science of designing airplanes and other machines that fly.

Altitude: the measurement of how high (or low) a plane is flying, in relation to the level of the sea or ground.

Biplane: a plane with two wings—an upper wing, and a lower wing—and a third wheel, or "taildragger."

Drag: the pressure created when a moving plane pushes against air; the pressure you feel while holding your hand outside the window of a moving car is an example of drag.

Crop duster: a plane (like Dusty!) that flies low and sprays nutrients on growing crops.

Flaps: moveable parts on the lower edge of the wing that are used to help the plane climb higher.

Floatplanes: planes that can land and take off from water as well as from dry land. Dusty becomes one of these when he is retrofitted with pontoons.

Fuselage: the long, main body of a plane.

Glider: a plane with no engine, powered by the force of the wind.

Gravity: the natural force that pulls objects—such as planes—toward the Earth.

Hangar: a plane garage.

Helicopter: a type of aircraft with rotors (rotating blades) on top that allow it to fly straight, up, down, and sideways . . . and even to hover in midair.

High-aspect-ratio wing: airplane wings that are long and narrow; some planes have wings that are short and wide (low-aspect-ratio wing).

Lift: the upward pressure created by air hitting an aircraft's wings during flight.

Piston engine: a machine powered by the rapid movement of a short cylinder within a tube of liquid or gas.

Pitch: the up-and-down movement a plane makes along its center of gravity when the nose rises or falls, based upon the movement of the plane's tail.

Pontoons: flotation devices that can make an airplane lighter than water.

Propeller: the rapidly rotating blades attached to an engine that assist in moving a plane forward, through the air.

Roll: the side-to-side movement of a plane when one wing tips down and the other wing tips up along its center of gravity.

Rudder: a movable tail fin, which controls a plane's movement from left to right (known as "yaw").

Smokejumper: a firefighter who parachutes down into a wildfire from a plane, enabling him to reach otherwise inaccessible areas.

Streamline: the design of an object that reduces drag, allowing air to move more smoothly across its surface.

Thrust: the force created by an engine, which pushes a plane through the air.

Transport plane: a very big airplane used to carry heavy machinery or cargo.

Turbine (jet) engine: a type of rotary machine that moves air and fuel through a set of fans, creating an exhaust strong enough to push the engine forward.

Weight: the natural gravitational force that pulls a plane toward the Earth.

Wing: one of two large flat parts that extend from either side of a plane's fuselage and help it to fly.

Yaw: the right-to-left movement of a plane when one wing moves forward and the other wing moves back along its center of gravity.